Reycraft Books
55 Fifth Avenue
New York, NY 10003

Reycraftbooks.com

Reycraft Books is a trade imprint and trademark of Newmark Learning, LLC.

Text © Adaiah Sanford

Educators and Librarians: Our books may be purchased in bulk for promotional, educational, or business use. Please contact sales@reycraftbooks.com.

Library of Congress Control Number: 2021921438

ISBN: 978-1-4788-7517-8

Author photo courtesy of Anette Sanford.
Illustrator photo courtesy of Ken Daley.

Printed in Dongguan, China. 8557/1221/18515

10 9 8 7 6 5 4 3 2 1

First Edition Hardcover published by Reycraft Books 2022.

Reycraft Books and Newmark Learning, LLC support diversity and the First Amendment, and celebrate the right to read.

REYCRAFT
B O O K S

The Legend of the Spirit Serpent

written by **Adaiah Sanford**

illustrated by **Ken Daley**

There was once a beautiful girl named Natari who lived in a small Kalinago village called Snake Cou. It was the home of the Great Spirit Serpent on the island of Dominica.

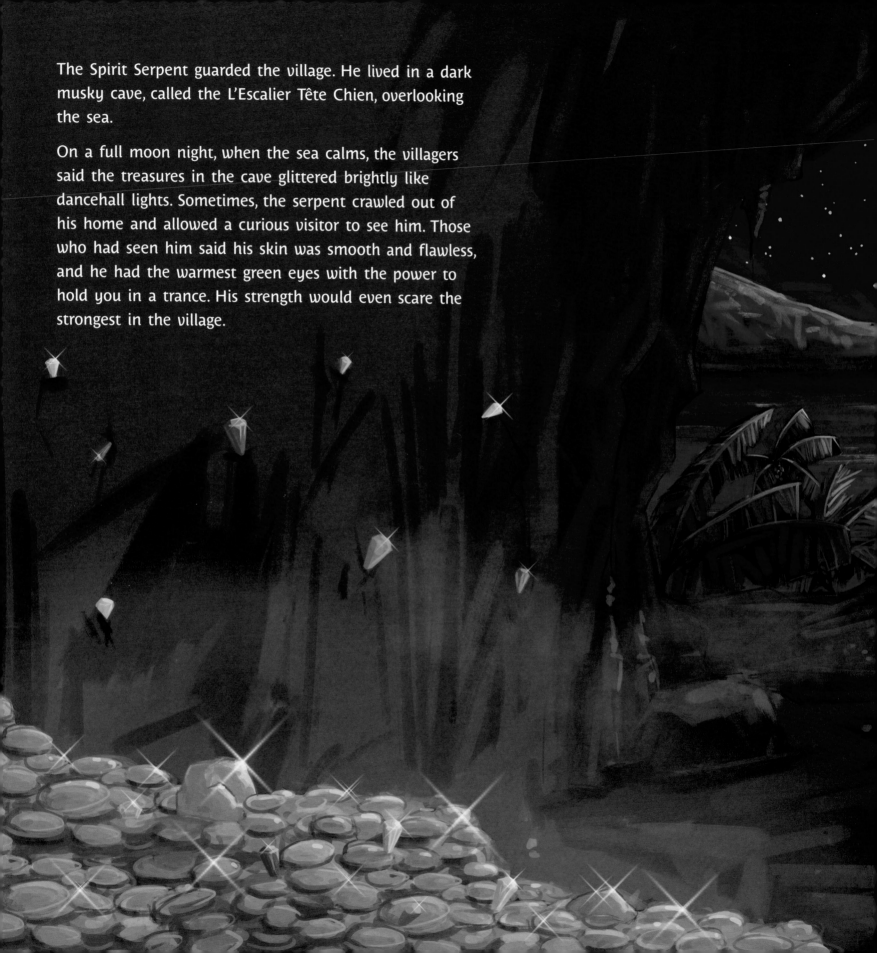

The Spirit Serpent guarded the village. He lived in a dark musky cave, called the L'Escalier Tête Chien, overlooking the sea.

On a full moon night, when the sea calms, the villagers said the treasures in the cave glittered brightly like dancehall lights. Sometimes, the serpent crawled out of his home and allowed a curious visitor to see him. Those who had seen him said his skin was smooth and flawless, and he had the warmest green eyes with the power to hold you in a trance. His strength would even scare the strongest in the village.

The serpent protected the tribe from evil forces that tried to destroy it—hurricanes, famine, and invaders. Many of the chiefs, upon returning from the Spirit Serpent's cave, showed off the precious jewels and treasures they were gifted. Natari's father even boasted of how the serpent helped him find his lovely wife.

Natari enjoyed adventures and longed to visit the Spirit Serpent's cave. But her mother never allowed it. Natari, who was only eight years old, was quite curious. What happened when the chief warrior went into the serpent's mysterious cave overlooking the sea? Natari wanted to know.

As an only child, Natari loved spending time with her father. He would train her like he did his warriors. It was something the other girls found rather amusing. They shouted "Tomboy" whenever they saw her.

It never bothered Natari. She loved that she could swim as good as any of the boys in her village, catch fish, hunt, row a canoe, and defend herself against the dangers of the wild.

One time her dad and his warriors went out to sea for many days. The women ran low on food. They became desperate for fear of starvation and sickness. So, Natari left for the woods. She came back with two wild agouti. Amazed, the village women rejoiced and prepared a feast.

When the men returned from sea, they saw the food. They were surprised when the women told them Natari had saved them from starvation. Natari's father felt proud. This act of bravery silenced the girls in the village. They never ridiculed Natari again. Instead, they tried to learn from her whenever they were in her presence.

Natari's confidence grew. She felt even more adventurous with each passing day. One day she took the courage to ask her father about the Spirit Serpent and what happened when he went into his cave.

"Only the leaders of the tribe can go in there, Natari. If anyone else ventures in, they will be swallowed alive by the Spirit Serpent," her father warned. But he happily told her of his experience. She didn't miss a word.

Her father explained that he would bring an offering of tobacco to the Spirit Serpent who, in return, would grant him anything he asked.

"Anything?" asked Natari, wide-eyed.

"Yes, anything," answered her father, showing her a gold bar that the Spirit Serpent had given him.

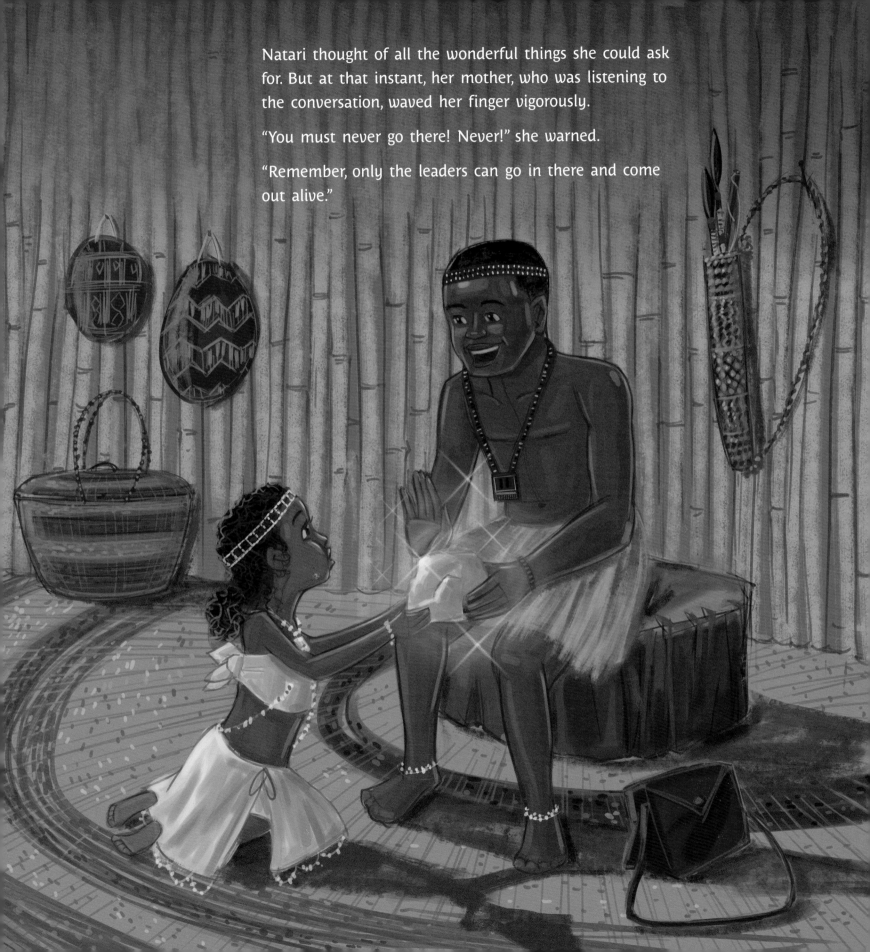

Natari thought of all the wonderful things she could ask for. But at that instant, her mother, who was listening to the conversation, waved her finger vigorously.

"You must never go there! Never!" she warned.

"Remember, only the leaders can go in there and come out alive."

"Why can't I be a leader?" Natari thought to herself. She had done enough to be a leader by saving the tribe from starvation. So, one evening on a full moon night while her parents were asleep, she sneaked out of their hut to explore the Spirit Serpent's cave.

The water sparkled brightly near the cave. The waves whispered a sweet melody as they stroked the rocks. Natari stood mesmerized as she saw bright, rainbow lights blinking from the entrance. For a moment, her mom's warning flashed through her mind. She

The sky shone clear and the moon sat at its peak, blazing down bright as day. The cave filled with the sounds of drums and people dancing.

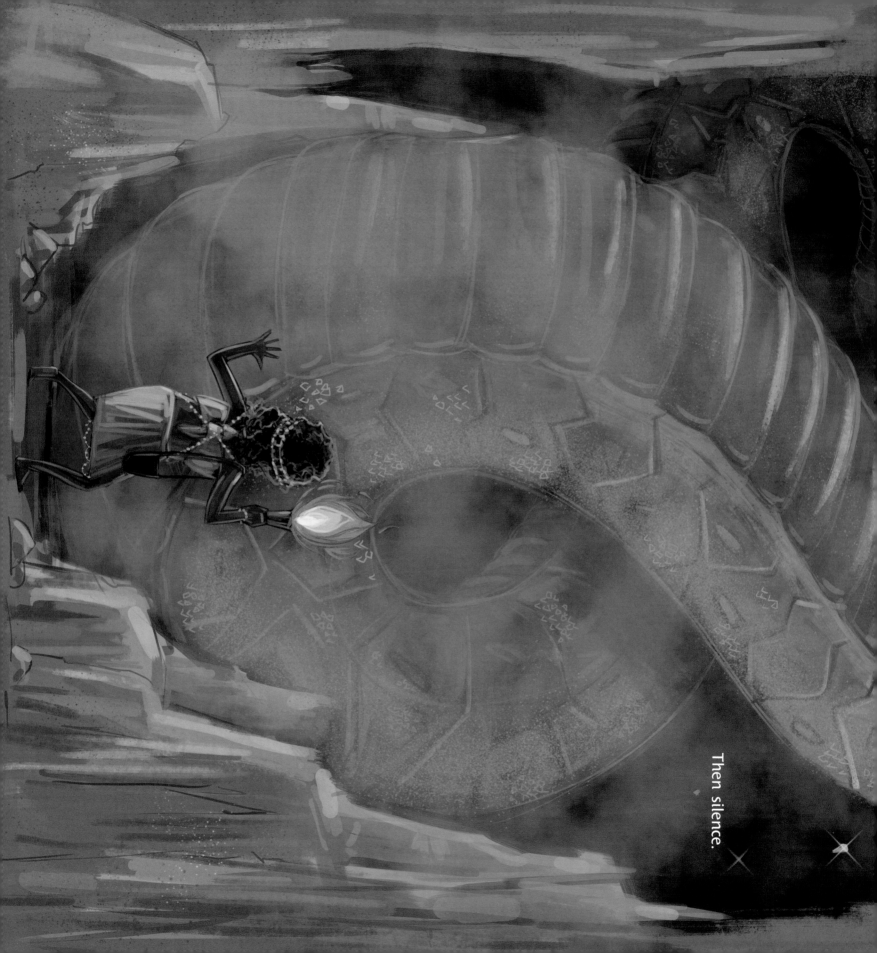

Then silence.

Suddenly she saw a swift movement. A force swept her off her feet, and she fell to the floor with a crack. Tinkling sounds rang from all around her. As she lifted her head, she saw treasure everywhere. She heard slithering but saw nothing. Natari shivered but her strong mind helped her remain still. A dark shadow blanketed her. Natari gasped as a huge blue and white snake looked down upon her. She wanted to run but her legs were numb.

The sounds of the drums returned.

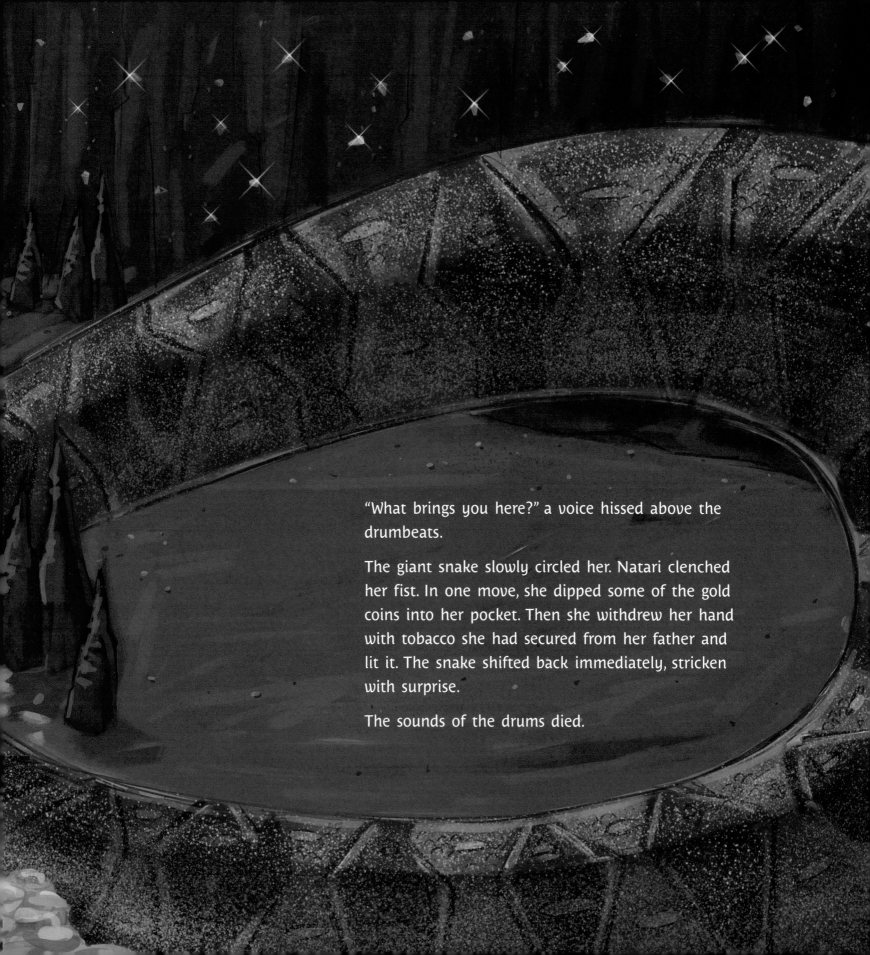

"What brings you here?" a voice hissed above the drumbeats.

The giant snake slowly circled her. Natari clenched her fist. In one move, she dipped some of the gold coins into her pocket. Then she withdrew her hand with tobacco she had secured from her father and lit it. The snake shifted back immediately, stricken with surprise.

The sounds of the drums died.

what brings you here?" the serpent hissed louder.

"I wish for you to spare my life and become my friend," Natari said,
looking into its green eyes, offering it the tobacco.

Her tender voice melted into the serpent. Slowly, it shrank
until it transformed into a boy. He had eyes and ears and
fingers and toes, as perfect as any human boy. She looked
upon him in wonder.

The strange boy seemed to be at a loss for words.

Then he whispered, "I've never had a human friend before. For generations, I have lived in this cave and have done as the people requested. I have granted them any wish that they asked for. The walls of this cave, and the ocean and animals that live here, are my friends."

Natari slowly walked to him and took his hands.

"Well, today you have a new friend in me," she assured him with her smile.

"Takahi tiya niri Natari."

"Friends don't steal from each other," the boy said and pulled away.

Natari dipped into her pocket
and emptied the coins onto the floor.

"You are right," she agreed.

The boy smiled, then walked with her to the outside
of the cave. There they spent the night calling the fishes.
The Spirit Serpent knew the names of each fish.

With a wave of his hand, he and Natari walked on water and looked at the other countries of the world through a magical window. She saw three huge ships sailing towards her land.

"Christopher Columbus is on his way to the Caribbean," the boy explained.

"This is my way of warning you of the things to come."

A sudden glimpse of the fate of the Kalinago tribe descended upon Natari. Before she could ask more of the boy, the rooster crowed. Natari knew her dad would soon be up to go hunting.

"Our secret?" Natari asked.

But before he could respond, she blurted out, "See you next time."

"Our secret and definitely next time," he replied.

Natari raced home and hopped through the window into her bed. A gold coin slipped from beneath her covers. She smiled as she fell asleep in a world of magical dreams with friendly serpents.

Adaiah Sanford

is the winner of the 1st Annual Caribbean Writer's Contest sponsored by Reycraft Books and the Ducreay Foundation. She lives on the island of Dominica. She is the youngest of five children and was born to parents of Kalinago descent. Adaiah's passion for writing books began in Kindergarten, where she made leaflets and scribbled stories within the pages. She started sharing Kalinago words via short videos on social media. Adaiah's passion for the revival of the Kalinago language resulted in her first book *The Beginner's Guide to the Kalinago Language*.

Ken Daley

is an artist from Canada. His parents emigrated there from the island of Dominica. His distinctive style expresses the vibrant spirit and culture of the Caribbean and the African diaspora. Ken's passion lies with stories that reflect his heritage as the child of immigrants, his connection to the Caribbean, and the richness and expanse of the African diaspora. He believes that diverse stories are essential to creating a more just and equitable world. As an award-winning illustrator, he is known for his use of bold colors and authentic details to depict Black life in all its iterations. He has illustrated many children's books, including *Joseph's Big Ride, Auntie Luce's Talking Paintings, A Feast for Joseph, In the Spirit of a Dream*, and *Jayden's Impossible Garden*.